RAJASTHAN

100 km
60 mi
PUNJAB
HARYANA
PAKISTAN
DELHI
UTTAR PRADESH
Sri Ganganagar
Hanumangarh
Churu
Bikaner
Jhunjhunu
Sikar
Alwar
Jaisalmer
Nagaur
Jaipur
Bharatpur
Dausa
Tilonia
Dholpur
Jodhpur
Karauli
Ajmer
Tonk
Sawai Madhopur
Barmer
Pali
Bhilwara
Bundi
Jalore
Rajsamand
Kota
Baran
Sirohi
Chittorgarh
Jhalawar
Udaipur
Pratapgarh
Dungarpur
Banswara
GUJRAT
MADHYA PRADESH

Arjun and his Village in India

Arjun and his village in India

Written and illustrated by

CAROL BARKER

VANI FOUNDATION
Connecting Indian languages, and world

VANI FOUNDATION

Connecting Indian languages, and world

4695, 21-A, Daryaganj, New Delhi 110 002

Phone : +91 11 23273167 Fax : +91 11 23275710

www.vanifoundation.org
foundationvani@gmail.com

Library Cataloguing in Publication Data

ARJUN AND HIS VILLAGE IN INDIA
by Carol Barker

(1) Rajasthan, India-Social Life and Customs Juvenile Literature
(2) Rural Village Life, Rajasthan-India Juvenile Literature

ISBN : 978-93-5229-075-8

First Published in 1979 by Oxford University Press
This Edition Published 2016 by Vani Foundation

Price : ₹ 295

Printed at Yash Printographics, Noida-201 301, Uttar Pradesh

Vani Foundation's signature motif is created by Artist S.H. Raza

This book is dedicated to
Bunker and Aruna Roy, Manya Jayaram-Lindsay,
also to Ram Kurran Ji, Ram Niwas Ji, Teja Ram-Ji,
Teena, Bata, Santosh, and to all my other friends in India.
And in remembrance of S. Shri-Niwasan (Vasu) 1949-2014
and Bhanwar Gopal (Bhurji) 1953 – 2004.

The rabi crop is sown in November and is harvested in March and April. This consists of wheat, barley, chick-peas, radishes, carrots, peas and mustard. During the summer months it is too dry and hot for anything to grow. But when the monsoon rains come in July and August the kharif crop is sown,—which is millet, maize and sesame seeds,—for vegetable oil—ground nuts, chillis and tomatoes. These are harvested in October and November.

It takes two men and two pairs of bullocks to keep the land watered. One man stands at the well-head. He lowers the leather pouch into the well, lets it fill with water, and then winds it up by pulley. The other man guides the two pairs of bullocks up and down the ramp, sitting on the rope. This rope is tied at one end to the leather pouch called a chadas and at the other end to the bullock's yoke. When the pouch gets to the top of the well-head, the water is tipped into the irrigation channels which run through the fields. This is called the Chadas System of Irrigation. The bullocks go round and round, up and down, and the water flows through the fields to the sound of singing. It is not just Ghisa-Baba who sings as he works at the well. All the farmers around Tilonia sing in the fields.

The sun begins to set at about 5 p.m., turning the sky red- gold as it sinks behind the mountains. This is the time when Arjun and Jamna Devi gather their goats together and drive them back to the village. Then they put the goats in their pen and give them a meal of berries. Aunts, uncles, brothers, sisters and cousins all return from the fields at this time, with the cart, the two pairs of bullocks, the cows and the buffaloes. The animals are put in their pens and all the family help to feed them with green-stuff, clover and grass—and for each cow and bullock a bowl of meal. Later the animals are milked, water is fetched and the family supper is cooked.

Arjun then has supper with his family, of wheat chapattis and liquid curd (like yogurt), and that is all he has to eat after his energetic day out in the 'jungle'. Then he fetches his bag of books and is off to school, with the other boys who have to help their families. Arjun goes to the Night School which is for children aged from six to fourteen. These schools were started by the Social Work & Research Centre [SWRC] in 1976, to enable children—who help their parents during the day-time, by taking their goats and other animals out to graze—to be able to go to school in the evening, and to get some education.

By 7 p.m. Arjun and his companions are in their classrooms, sitting cross-legged in a circle on the floor with their slates balanced on their knees and their chalks ready to write. Each room is lit by several oil-lamps which cast a glow on the boys' faces peering from under their turbans.

At home and with his friends and family Arjun speaks a local language called Marwari. At this school they learn to read and write in Hindi, which is the main language spoken in Northern India. They learn about the history and geography of India, and how it is governed today: about Rajasthan and Tilonia in particular, and about farming and how to look after animals. They also do maths and health education and hygiene, and learn which vegetables they should eat to keep well and stay strong.

When I asked Arjun one day about his school, he said, 'I enjoy it. I like maths best, especially multiplication tables—if you're good at maths the money-lenders can't cheat you! School helps me. It's good to be able to read and write too, because then nobody can make a fool of you.'

School for Arjun finishes at 9 p.m. He goes home and is in bed by 10 p.m. His day is long, and he always sleeps soundly after it.

In Tilonia village most people follow the Hindu religion. In the past Hindus were divided into four main castes in India. The Brahmins and Kshatriyas were the two upper castes, then there were the middle and lower castes, the Vaisyas and the Sudras. The castes were divided according to the people's occupations, or work. The Brahmins were the first and highest caste. They were the priests, [who wore the sacred thread] and were religious leaders, and teachers of the people.

The Kshatriyas were the second highest caste. They were the martial, or military caste,—the Kings,—who were Rajputs. They were brave generals and military men—like the Maharajas of Jaipur and the Maharanas of Udaipur, who rode on horseback leading their armies of horses and elephants into battle against the marauding Kings from neighbouring states, to defend their great forts and palaces, and their people.

However, after Indian independence, the government stopped providing the Maharajas with financial support. Therefore today the Maharajas have lost their political power and wealth. Many of the great forts and palaces [like Mehrangarh Fort in Jodhpur, and the City Palace in Udaipur] in Rajasthan have been turned into national museums. Also many of the palaces have been turned into hotels, and the Maharajas have become successful businessman.

The Vaisyas, the third caste, were the traditional trading community of merchants, shopkeepers and businessmen. Among them were the Banias, moneylenders and Sonars, or silversmiths. The Sudras were the fourth traditional caste, which included labourers and artisans. They are now called Dalits, and they include many different groups of people who work as weavers, washer-men, drummers, musicians, all the leatherworkers, blacksmiths, sweepers and others.

In the past the traditional Hindu caste system was extremely rigid, and it was almost impossible for someone from the Dalit caste to improve their situation and get a better job. However, in the last twenty to thirty years,—from 1984 to 2014,—there have been huge social and economic changes. There are now moneylenders and businessmen in every caste.

People from the Dalit caste are now able to get a better education. They can borrow money from the banks, and set up their own businesses, for example in the marble and stone business, and in the clothes business, and can now make a decent living.

Today the government has divided people into four groups. Firstly, the General Castes, including Brahmins, Rajputs and Banias. Secondly, Other Backward Castes, including Jats,—the farmers,—Kumhars,—the potters,—Nais,—the barbers,—and Khati,—the carpenters,—and others. Thirdly, the Scheduled Castes, who are now called Dalits,—which now includes many groups of people doing different kinds of work [as mentioned before]. And fourthly, there are Scheduled Tribes, like the Bhil and Meena people.

The Government of India has now passed laws to help poor people from the Dalit and Scheduled Castes, including men and women, to enable them to get government jobs, and reserved places on the Village Councils, known as the Panchayat.

In Tilonia village there is a woman named Kamla, who comes from the Dalit caste, who traditionally worked as weavers. She was elected by the majority of the people in Tilonia to become Sarpanch, the leader of the Village Council. This was an absolute triumph, both from the social point of view, as she came from the Dalit caste, and because she had succeeded as a woman, to be elected as head of the Panchayat, which has traditionally always been a position held by a man. So there are important social and economic changes that are taking place.

In the main street in Tilonia the Banias have a store where they sell cloth and grain, soap and cooking oil, and many other things. The Sonars have their shops in which silver and jewellery are displayed. Men, women, children and animals weave to and fro through the narrow streets. The busiest times are in the early morning and the evening, when the farmers and their families go to and from their work in the fields.

Most people in India are Hindus. Hindus believe in hundreds of different gods and goddesses, to whom they have built many temples and shrines. The most important of them are the gods Brahma, Vishnu and Shiva, the goddesses Parvati and Lakshmi, and Ganesa, the elephant god, and Hanuman, the monkey god.

Brahma is the Creator. Vishnu is the Protector. He changes himself into many forms that are also gods, like Krishna around whom there are legends of love and much poetry written and whose skin is dark blue. He is also Rama, the brave and famous prince, the power of goodness who prevailed over evil when he slew the demon King Ravana in the epic legend, the Ramayana. Shiva is the God of the Dance (the Life-Force) but he is also the Destroyer. Lakshmi is Vishnu's wife, and she is the Goddess of Wealth. Parvati is married to Shiva. She is Shakti (that is Energy, the Life- Force) and she has a fierce form as Kali, the destroyer of evil, war and disease. As Durga, Parvati is usually shown as a beautiful lady riding a tiger or a lion.

Shiva and Parvati had a son called Karttikeya. Now Shiva was in the habit of going away for long periods to sit meditating on a mountain in the Himalayas. One legend relates how Parvati was having a bath during one of these absences and she modeled a child out of a body-scrub called 'ubtan', —which is made of lentil powder mixed with oil. She called him Ganesa. One day, when Ganesa was over a year old, Parvati asked him to guard the door while she took her bath, to make sure nobody disturbed her. It happened that on that day Shiva returned after his long absence. Ganesa did not know who he was, and when he saw him he said, 'You are not allowed in. My mother is having her bath.' Shiva was so furious at this that he cut off the boy's head with his sword. 'You don't know what you have done,' cried Parvati. 'You have killed my youngest son!' Stricken by grief, Shiva straightaway went out to look for another head for Ganesa. The first creature he met was an elephant. He chopped off its head, hurried back and placed the head on young Ganesa's body. Immediately the boy sprang to life again. So that is why Ganesa has an elephant's head on a human body.

One day Shiva wished to put his two children to the test to find out which of them would marry first. He invited them both to make a circle round the earth as quickly as they could. The eldest son Karttikeya mounted his peacock and made off at once with all speed. But Ganesa, taking his time about it, respectfully made a circle round his parents. When Shiva asked him why he did this, Ganesa replied, 'It is said in the Rig Vedas that he who honours his parents by circling round them seven times has as much honour as he who circles the earth seven times.' And so he was the winner in the test.

Ganesa is one of the most popular Hindu gods. He is the god of good luck, and the remover of obstacles. He is also the patron of learning and helps people to gain wealth and success. When Hindus do their Puja, or worship, they must pray to Ganesa first before all the other gods. They light incense to him and bring offerings of flowers, coconuts, fruits and betel-nuts on leaves.

As well as the national gods and goddesses that people worship all over India, there are local gods and heroes. One of the most important of these in Rajasthan is Tejaji, a warrior hero to whom there are many shrines in Tilonia. Tejaji is said to have been born in Kharnal in Rajasthan. He was the son of a king, but both his parents died when he was a baby, and he was left in a field, wrapped in a cloth. A peasant woman found the baby and he was brought up by the farmer and his wife.

One day many years later when Tejaji was working in the fields, the farmer's wife came to him with his food, and said, 'If you want to eat bread prepared by the hand of a bride with red-painted hands, go to the house of your father-in-law and bring home your bride.'

So Tejaji went to the carpenter to get a cart made, bought a pair of bullocks and set out with some of his friends to fetch his bride. On the way they saw two cobras being burnt in a fire. Tejaji took pity on them and managed to save one of the cobras from the flames. The cobra then insisted that it would have to bite Tejaji for not saving the other cobra too. So Tejaji promised to return to that place.

Then Tejaji went to the home of his father-in-law and was married to his beautiful daughter Sundar. But before he could take her to his home he said he had a duty to perform. On his way back to the place of the cobras he met an old lady in distress. 'Robbers have stolen my bullocks,' she cried. 'Will you go and get them back for me?' So Tejaji ran after the

robbers and attacked them. Though he was wounded with sword-cuts from head to foot he fought so bravely that he drove the robbers off, recaptured the bullocks and gave them back to the old lady. Then, true to his word, he returned to the cobra. The cobra was waiting to bite Tejaji, but when it saw his body covered with wounds, it hesitated. Brave Tejaji held out his tongue. The cobra bit it. Tejaji was poisoned by the bite and fell down and died.

It is said that Tejaji was given the power of restoring to life people bitten by snakes. So people who have been bitten come to his shrines today. They tie a thread round their right foot as they repeat the name of Tejaji. Then they light incense and the priest sucks out the venom from the bite. 'With the help of the power of Tejaji the person is always cured,' I was assured.

In Sursura, the town in which he died, there is a big statue and shrine to Tejaji. There is a fair held there every year, when thousands of people come to worship Tejaji and enjoy the Tejaji Mela. On the day of the Mela a live cobra on a large bronze plate is placed in somebody's house. Pilgrims come with little earthenware dishes of milk which they offer to the cobra. They light incense and ask for the cobra's blessing. They believe that Tejaji has come to help them in the form of this live snake.

As there are many Indian gods and goddesses, there are many religious festivals every year. There are national festivals like Divali and Holi, and local festivals for the local gods and heroes. One of these is the festival of Ghasbabba, the God of Protection for Tilonia, which takes place once a year.

On the evening of the day of this festival, the people of Tilonia dress up in their best clothes. The men and boys put on new brightly-coloured turbans of crimson red, purple or saffron yellow, with fresh white dhotis and shirts. The women and girls dress in brilliant shawls, veils, blouses and skirts of red, yellow and purple, patterned with gold thread, embroidery and sequins. They decorate their hair and wear all their finest jewellery—earrings, necklaces, nose-rings, bracelets, anklets and toe-rings, so that they glitter like queens. At about 9.30 p.m., when it is dark, people leave their homes and walk in procession to the edge of the village. The men and boys go in front, with the women and girls behind, singing together. Male drummers,

specially hired for the occasion, beat out their rhythms. The people gather round a black stone, which is mounted on two blocks of wood, and has been painted white for the occasion. Torchbearers come with flaming torches, and some people carry lamps to light up the scene.

The Brahmin priest stands by the stone. The drum-beats and the women's singing dies down. The priest says some mantras, or prayers, and then holds out a mirror in front of two eyes painted on the stone. At this point the mirror shatters into pieces and it is said that the spirit of Ghasbabba, the God of Protection, enters into the stone. Everyone drums and sings, and the first of several pairs of bullocks that are ready is harnessed to the stone. It is a great honour for a farmer who has oxen big and strong enough to pull it.

The stone is heaved on to a wooden base and dragged round the village. The bullocks are changed regularly because of the weight of the stone and because other farmers want the honour of pulling it. At the head of the procession are the bullocks driven by the farmer, then the priest walking behind, followed by crowds of happy people singing and drumming.

People believe that in this way Ghasbabba the God, who has entered the stone, protects the animals from diseases and blesses the men, women and children in and around Tilonia village, so that they are all healthy and happy for another year.

Arjun thoroughly enjoys festivals like this one. But it only happens once a year. 'I like music and songs,' he said to me one day, 'and I like going to Bhajans.' A Bhajan is a gathering of the villagers, mostly men, older women and children, at which there are music and drums and singing. It is not a festival but a get-together to sing praises to the gods. Bhajans go on all night. Arjun explained that the songs are usually by Mira, who sang songs in praise of Lord Krishna. The villagers also sing to Lord Rama.

I asked Arjun if he wanted to get married. 'Nai,' he said, 'I don't want to. When I grow up I want to be a farmer, and specially to work at the well. And I want to have four bullocks of my own.'

INDIA

NORTHERN AREAS
SHAKSAM VALLEY
SIACHEN GLACIER
AKSAI CHIN
Srinagar
JAMMU AND KASHMIR
AZAD KASHMIR
0 200 400 Kilometers
0 200 400 Miles
HIMACHAL PRADESH
Simla
PUNJAB
Chandigarh
Dehra Dun
UTTAR-ANCHAL
HARYANA
Delhi
DELHI
New Delhi
ARUNACHAL PRADESH
SIKKIM
UTTAR PRADESH
Itanagar
Gangtok
Rajasthan
Jaipur
Lucknow
Dispur
ASSAM
NAGALAND
Kohima
Patna
Shillong
MEGHALAY
MANIPUR
BIHAR
Imphal
Agartala
JHARKHAND
WEST BENGAL
TRIPURA
Aizawl
MIZORAM
Gandhinager
Ranchi
Bhopal
Kolkata (Catcutta)
GUJARAT
MADHYA PRADESH
CHHATTISGARH
Raipur
Diu
Daman
Shvassa
MAHARASHTRA
Bhubaneshwar
DAMAN AND DIU
DADRD AND NAGAR HAVELI
ORISSA
Mumbai (Bombay)
TELANGANA
Bay of Bengal
Hyderabad
PONDICHERRY
Panaji
GOA
ANDHAR PRADESH
Arabian Sea
KARNATAKA
Chennai (Madras)
Bangalore
Port Blair
PONDICHERRY
Cuddalore
Kavaratti
TAMIL NADL
PONDICHERRY
KERALA
ANDAMAN AND NICOBAR ISLANDS
LAKSHADWEEP
Trivandrum
Indian Ocean